Caroline Grégoire was born in 1970 in Namur, Belgium, and currently lives in Spa. Her enthusiasm for children's books, painting and color led her to her career as an author, illustrator and graphic designer. Books aren't the only place her work can be seen; she's designed four Belgian postage stamps.

Also by Caroline Grégoire
Counting with Apollo (Kane/Miller 2004)

First American Paperback Edition 2006
First American Edition 2002
by Kane/Miller Book Publishers, Inc.
La Jolla, California

Originally published in 1999 in Germany under the title **Apollo – rundrum schön!**
By Baumhaus Verlag AG, Frankfurt am Main, Germany

Copyright ©1999 by Baumhaus Verlag AG
American text ©2002 by Kane/Miller Book Publishers, Inc.

Library of Congress Cataloging-in-Publication Data:
Grégoire, Caroline
[Apollo, rundrum schön. English]
Apollo/Caroline Grégoire – 1st American ed.   p.cm.
Summary: The owner of a dachshund describes how adorable, obedient, and clever
his dog is from all sides and all directions.
ISBN 1-929132-23-9
[1. Dachshunds – Fiction. 2. Dogs – Fiction. 3. Space perception – Fiction.] I.Title
PZ7.G8544 Ap 2002   [E] – dc21   2001038864

Printed and bound in China by Regent Publishing Services, Ltd.

2 3 4 5 6 7 8 9 10

ISBN: 978-1-933605-04-3

Apollo

Caroline Grégoire

Kane/Miller

BOOK PUBLISHERS

Would you like to meet my best friend? His name is Apollo.

Back

This is his cute little bottom, and his tail, which is always wagging...

Mid

...his long,

dle

hin body...

Front

...and his delightful little sausage nose.

This is Apollo from the **side**.
Isn't he just adorable?

From the
front
he's adorable...

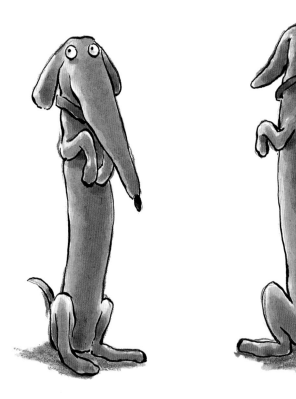

...and from the
back he's
adorable, too.

from below

He's still adorable!

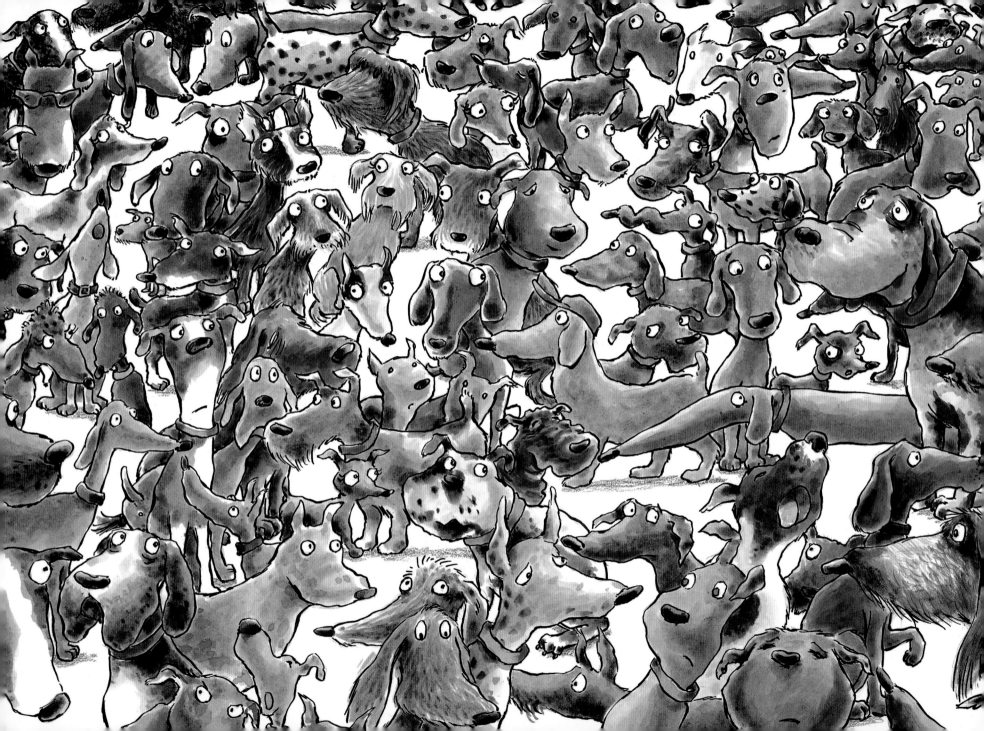

In a crowd

you can always spot Apollo.
He's the most adorable!

Alone

There is no question: he's too adorable for words.
But Apollo is more than just a pretty face...

Apollo is also very
well-trained.
He does everything you say.

horizontally

vertically

And here's your reward, Apollo!

diagonally

left

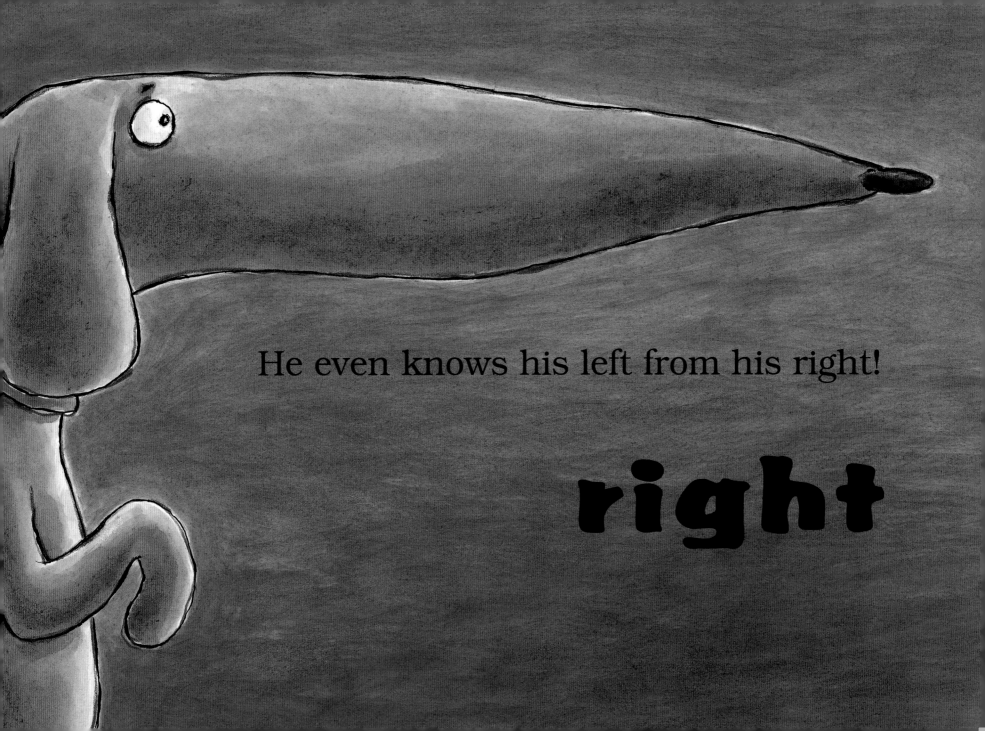

He even knows his left from his right!

right

Apollo is the most adorable, the most obedient, the most clever dog in the whole wide world. He can also do magic tricks...

1/2

...ta-da! Apollo is in half!

Different halves!

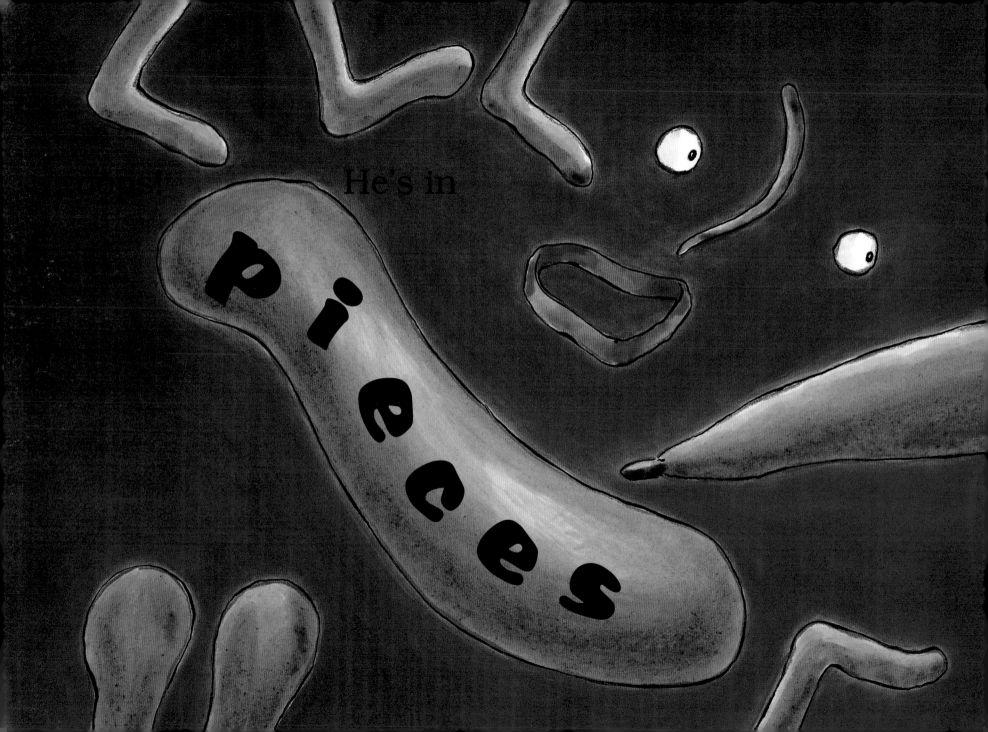

whole

...ta-da! Oh, no!
Something went wrong with that trick!

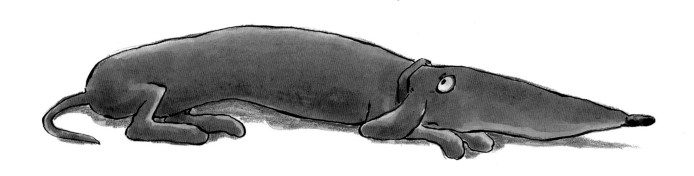

But even a Super Dog gets tired.
It's time for his nap.

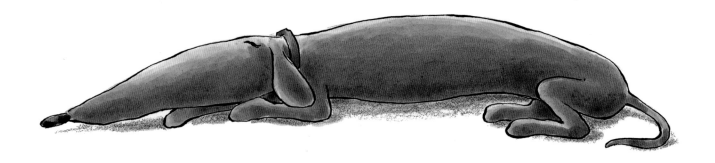